For Evan and George with love – M. R.

With love to Barbara and David – N. E.

PUFFIN BOOKS

UK | USA | Canada | Ireland | Australia | India | New Zealand | South Africa

Puffin Books is part of the Penguin Random House group of companies whose addresses
can be found at global. penguinrandomhouse. com.

www.penguin.co.uk   www.puffin.co.uk   www.ladybird.co.uk

First published 2013. This edition published 2014

002

Text copyright © Michelle Robinson, 2013
Illustrations copyright © Nick East, 2013
All rights reserved
The moral right of the author and illustrator has been asserted

Printed in China

The authorized representative in the EEA is Penguin Random House Ireland, Morrison
Chambers, 32 Nassau Street, Dublin D02 YH68

A CIP catalogue record for this book is available from the British Library

ISBN: 978-0-723-29646-1

All correspondence to:
Puffin Books, Penguin Random House Children's
One Embassy Gardens, 8 Viaduct Gardens, London SW11 7BW

FSC
www.fsc.org

MIX
Paper from
responsible sources
FSC® C018179

Goodnight Tractor

PUFFIN

Michelle Robinson

Illustrated by **Nick East**

The stars are out.
It's time for bed.
So say 'goodnight',
my sleepyhead.

Goodnight farmer.
Goodnight plough.

Goodnight trailer.

Goodnight cow.

Goodnight dog

nd goodnight sheep . . .

Goodnight tractor, time to sleep.

Goodnight combine.

Goodnight truck.

Goodnight
donkey.

Goodnight duck.

Goodnight pig,
    and goodnight sheep . . .

Goodnight tractor, time to sleep

Goodnight wagon.
Goodnight puddles.

Goodnight horse
and hens in huddles.

Dog and donkey, duck and cow.

Combine, wagon, truck and plough.

Oinks

and brays

and moos

and baas.

Quacks
and
neighs,
and moon and stars.

Goodnight all,

now count the sheep . . .

Goodnight tractor, time to sleep.